How Dogs Came from Wolves

Scientists Probe 12 Animal Mysteries

How Dogs Came from Wolves

and Other Explorations of Science in Action

Jack Myers, Ph.D.
Senior Science Editor
HIGHLIGHTS FOR CHILDREN

Illustrated by John Rice

Boyds Mills Press

Photo credits: page 16: John Fenwick; page 26: Gregory S. Stone; page 51: Arthur L. DeVries.

Illustration and graphic artwork credits: page 17—based on data of J. Neitz, T. Geist, and G.H. Jacobs; page 30—based on data of F.N. White and J.L. Kinney; page 38—based on a map published in *Nature*, February 22, 1990 (volume 343, page 746); page 60—based on data and illustration published in *Electric Fishes* by P. Moller.

Published by Caroline House
Boyds Mills Press, Inc.
A Highlights Company
815 Church Street
Honesdale, Pennsylvania 18431
Printed in China
Visit our web site at: www.boydsmillspress.com

U.S. Cataloging-in-Publication Data
    (Library of Congress Standards)

Myers, Jack.
    How dogs came from wolves : and other explorations of science in action : scientists probe 12 animal mysteries / by Jack Myers ; illustrated by John Rice.— 1st ed.
 [64] p. : col. ill. ; cm.
Includes bibliographical references and index.
Intriguing questions about animals are answered by scientists in these twelve explorations taken from the award-winning column in *Highlights for Children*.
ISBN 1-56397-411-8
1. Animals — Miscellanea — Juvenile literature. 2. Zoology — Research — Juvenile literature. 3. Animals — Miscellanea. 4. Zoology — Research — Miscellanea. I. Rice, John, ill. II. Title.
590 21 2001 CIP
00-112337

First edition, 2001
The text of this book is set in 13-point Berkeley.

10 9 8 7 6 5 4 3 2 1

CONTENTS

Introduction

Science is the search for understanding of our world. All the fun and excitement is in the search. That's where the action is. That's why this series of books is called Science in Action. It tells about explorations and discoveries as they happened.

All of these explorations have appeared in *Highlights for Children*. Earlier they were called Science Reporting. That was also a good title because each is based on an original and current report cited on page 62.

Most of these chapters tell about the scientific detective work that gave us answers to some great questions of pure curiosity. In some cases, new findings were made since my account was published in *Highlights*. I have updated and revised them as needed.

The illustrations are by John Rice, who has had long experience in picturing wildlife in natural settings. At the beginning of most chapters, he has slipped in just-for-fun illustrations to tell something about the ideas of the articles. Then his main illustrations will help you think about the animals themselves.

This volume contains discoveries about animals, their behavior, and the parts they play in nature. Please follow with me in the tracks of the scientists who made the discoveries.

Welcome to Science in Action.

Jack Myers

Jack Myers, Ph.D.
Senior Science Editor
Highlights for Children

Elephant Talk

Scientists discovered how to listen in.

Elephants are highly social animals. In Africa, they live together in groups of related females with their calves, often led by the grandmother of the family. When the males reach their teens, they become independent. Adult males live in separate bachelor herds or alone, often visiting with many families.

Scientists naturally expected that animals living so closely together would have a lot of communication. They had listened to sounds of an elephant herd. But until recently no one had heard what could be called elephant talk.

Katy Payne is a scientist in the Bioacoustics Research Program of the Laboratory of Ornithology at Cornell University. The laboratory is famous for its study of birds. The program was started to study bird songs but has gone on to include many other animal sounds. That's the bioacoustics part.

Katy had been studying the songs and other sounds of whales. She was curious also about other big social animals and was excited when she got a chance to spend a week with elephants at the zoo in Portland, Oregon.

She spent every day of that week watching and listening to elephants. "Elephants may not have been the only interesting animals in the zoo, but I had eyes, or ears, only for them," she wrote later.

She also learned from the zookeepers, who told her about some of the things their elephants had done. She began to think of those elephants as individuals, each with its own personality.

Katy had gotten hooked on elephants. On her way home from that first experience, she realized how little she had learned about elephant talk.

Could it be that the elephants were talking in sounds that her ears couldn't hear? Some whales are known to do that. And she remembered several times in the elephant house when she had sensed a throbbing in the air—something she felt but couldn't hear.

Infrasound

When she got home, Katy told other scientists in the program about her idea. They encouraged her and found equipment she could use to record *infrasound*—sound below the frequency that human ears can hear.

In a few months Katy and two friends were back at the elephant house with special microphones and tape recorders. While the recorders were running, the researchers watched and kept records of what was going on.

In the laboratory they played back the tapes, but at ten times the recording speed. That increased the frequency of the recorded sounds so people could hear them. Now there was a lot to hear—Katy says it sounded like a bunch of cows in a barn. She had learned how to listen to elephant talk.

Now that Katy had learned about infrasound, she wondered how wild African elephants actually talked to one another. That question took her to East Africa and the Amboseli National Park of Kenya.

There she teamed up with two scientists who knew each of the several hundred elephants in the park. By watching elephants while recording their sounds, the team was able to figure out several different calls.

When two related elephant families met, there was a lot of excitement, with trumpeting, screaming, and special rumbles of *greeting*. There was a *let's-go* call used by an elephant that seemed to want the family to get moving. There were *contact* calls used by an elephant that had wandered off and wanted to locate her family. In response there were *answering* calls from the family.

Katy could hear the calls of nearby elephants without the help of recording devices because they included some higher-frequency sounds. These calls don't travel as far as infrasound does.

Katy also recorded many distant, low-frequency calls.

She guessed that the elephants relied upon these infrasonic calls for long-range communication.

To find out whether the guess was right, the team reversed procedure. They used loudspeakers mounted on a truck to play back elephant recordings while they watched a group of elephants from a tower at a watering hole.

When an elephant heard a distant call, it had a special listening response. It stood still, spread its ears, and moved its head from side to side as if locating the direction of the call. By moving the loudspeakers to different locations, the researchers found that elephants stopped to listen to calls played back from more than a mile away.

The Cool Evenings

The scientists also found that elephants do most of their calling in late afternoon or early evening. At that time the ground is cooling. The air above forms a cool layer close to the ground. That layering of air creates a kind of "sound channel" that can carry sounds for great distances. At this time of day, calls probably can be heard by elephants even as far as five miles away.

The curiosity and hard work of Katy Payne has led to the beginnings of an understanding of how elephants talk to one another. As for Katy, she has really been hooked on elephants ever since.

Do Dogs See in Color?

To find out, scientists taught them a game.

We often wonder whether other animals see the world the way we see it. Do they see in color? That sounds like a simple question, but it's a hard one to answer. It is often supposed that animals such as dogs and cats do not have color vision. In fact, you can find that as a statement in some books. Now we have had some experiments to help us really find out.

We usually think of colors as lined up in order. That special order is not one that anyone invented. It's the order in which they occur when white light is broken into its colors, as in a rainbow or when light goes through a prism. That whole color lineup is called a *spectrum*. Color depends on the wavelength of light, which we measure in *nanometers*. A nanometer (nm) is a billionth of a meter. The color spectrum visible to humans runs from 400 nm (blue) to about 700 nm (red).

How Eyes See Color

To help us understand how dogs see, we need to think about how our own eyes see light and color. At the back of the eye is a filmy layer called the retina. It contains millions of light-sensitive cells, each connected to the brain by a nerve pathway. So the eye and brain are always giving us a built-in picture.

Actually, there are two types of light-sensitive cells. One type, the *rods*, work only in dim light and don't help us see color. The other type, the *cones*, come in three different kinds. Each kind is tuned to one of three colors: blue, yellow, or red. You can see why we can speak about three primary colors. Any other color, including white, can be made by adjusting the amounts of blue, yellow, and red light. You can see color because of your blue-, yellow-, and red-sensitive cones.

A Game to Test Vision

What about an animal like a dog? Does a dog see colors? Or does it see everything in different shades of white to gray to black? You can't ask a dog what color it sees when you turn on blue light. And if it can see a difference between two colors, such as blue and yellow, it might choose yellow just because yellow looks brighter, not because it can actually see color. It takes careful experiments to find out whether a dog has color vision.

A recent study on dogs used a lot of experiments. First the dogs were taught a game that they could play over and over. The game was played in a box with three small windows in one wall. These were lighted from the outside by either white light or by chosen colors, so that two windows were alike and one was different.

A two-color eye system like the dog's has been found also in cats and squirrels. It may be common in mammals. A three-color eye system like most humans' has been found in chimpanzees, goldfish, and pigeons. There is still a lot to be learned about animal color vision.

For each dog, the game was to pick the window that looked different and then touch that one with its nose. If the dog made the right choice, a beef-and-cheese treat dropped down. After a wrong choice there was no treat, only a buzzer and a new combination of windows for the next game.

Once the dogs were trained, they would play the game several hundred times each day. The whole apparatus was controlled by a computer that also kept track of results.

For the games of the first experiments, all three windows were lighted equally by white light. One window also received a weak colored light. If a dog correctly picked the window with added color, it got the treat. The game was repeated again and again, each time with a smaller amount of added color. Then the series was repeated for twenty-one

Sensitivity to Different Colors

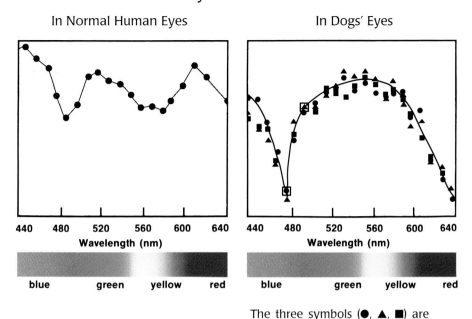

In Normal Human Eyes   In Dogs' Eyes

Wavelength (nm)   Wavelength (nm)

blue   green   yellow   red   blue   green   yellow   red

The three symbols (●, ▲, ■) are
for three different dogs.

other colors that differed slightly from blue through red.

The idea was to find out how sensitive the dogs were to different colors. The results for three dogs in the study are shown in the graph above. You can see that the dogs were much alike because the three symbols are close together for each color. All dogs were most sensitive to color at the high points: at about 440 nm (blue) and about 560 nm (yellow). They were least sensitive at the low points: 480 nm (blue-green) and 640 nm (red).

The Dog's Color Vision

The graph says that a dog can tell the difference between colors like blues and greens and yellows. But a dog is not very good at seeing reds. Dogs' eyes must be different from yours. They have only two kinds of receptors, one tuned to blue and one tuned to yellow. All the colors a dog can see can be made from some mixture of blue and yellow.

Most people have eyes with three kinds of cones. Our world of color is made up of mixtures of blue, yellow, and red. Some people do not see all colors so well. About one person in twenty is partly color-blind, most often because their red-sensitive cones are missing. And you can say that about a dog's eyes, too.

So the answer is: Dogs do have color vision, but they are color-blind to reds. If you make stop signs for dogs, don't use red.

How Dogs Came from Wolves

People bred tame animals from wild ones.

Dogs have been living with people for thousands of years. That's a special relationship. How did it start? And where did dogs come from?

The search for answers takes us so far into the past that there are no written records. Scientists have been piecing together different kinds of clues. Some clues come from studies of how people lived more than ten thousand years ago, in the Stone Age. At that time, people made a living by gathering plant roots and seeds and by hunting.

Our oldest clue about the domestication of dogs is the discovery of wolf bones buried together with human bones in a cave that people lived in about fourteen thousand years ago. Dog bones and wolf bones are much alike. But we can tell them apart, mainly because wolves have narrower snouts and jaws.

So it seems that over time the wolf became a dog after it began living with people. It was the first kind of animal to be domesticated and the only one, except the cat, to be commonly taken into people's homes as a pet.

Why Choose Wolves?

Of all the animals out there, why did people pick wolves? Wolves are not often thought of as likely pets.

However, wolves are like people in important ways. They live in packs and join together in hunting. They have ways of communicating with one another. And they have social customs for getting along together—such as following a pack leader.

The first step in domestication could have happened without any planning at all. Hanging around a Stone Age hunting camp and living on scraps left by people would have been an easy way for a wolf to make a living. It's also easy to imagine a child bringing home a lost cub: "Mom, can I keep it?"

For later steps in the history of dogs, people must have been in charge. They picked the wolves that could stay in camp. We suppose that by keeping only the tamer wolves

and controlling their mating, people were beginning what we now call animal *breeding*. They were selecting wolves for the built-in, inherited characteristics they wanted. They were making dogs out of wolves.

Over the course of time, people found many dog characteristics that could be chosen or improved by selective breeding. Today we have more than four hundred kinds, or *breeds*, of dogs ranging from little Pekingese and Chihuahuas to Great Danes and Saint Bernards.

Breeding Foxes

The many breeds of dogs show that selective breeding can be used to make great changes in their inherited physical characteristics. Does that also work for the early steps of domestication? Can we really use selective breeding to make a tame animal out of a wild one? In 1959 a Russian scientist, Dmitry Belyaev, began an experiment to find out. The experiment is still going on today under his student, Lyudmila Trut.

The animals chosen for the experiment were silver foxes. Like other foxes, they are *canids*, members of the "doglike" family of animals. Foxes had never been domesticated. Also,

they were easy to get because they were already being raised on farms to provide furs for fur coats. Foxes raised that way are still wild—snarly, easily scared, and ready to bite.

The experiment started with 130 foxes and was designed to ask a simple question: What will happen if they are bred and selected for tameness? The scientists had a rule against playing with their foxes. That way the experiment would show only the effects of selective breeding.

Tameness Test

In each new litter, each new generation, the pups were regularly tested for tameness as they grew up. The experimenters used a test of offering food by hand to a pup while trying to pet it. In the first litters, most foxes would run away or try to bite the experimenter. Only a few pups became tame enough to take food from a hand or allow themselves to be petted.

Even fewer of those tame puppies were still tame when they grew up to be adults. It is generally observed that many wild animals can be tamed when young but become wild again when they grow up. Tameness is sometimes called a juvenile characteristic. It is almost as if selecting for tameness is selecting for those animals that "never grow up."

Only the tamest foxes from each generation were selected to breed with one another. In later generations the number of tame adults kept increasing. Today, after only thirty-five generations, almost 80 percent of the adult foxes pass the "tame test." Many even show the friendliness of dogs, wagging their tails and whining to get attention.

Though Dr. Belyaev's experiment is still going on, it has already shown us about a key event in domestication. By selective breeding over many generations, a snarly wild animal has become tame enough to be a house pet.

The Long-Distance Whale

It's the very same whale. You can tell by its tail.

A humpback whale has set a long-distance migration record for mammals. That record all by itself isn't very important. But it shows that scientists are learning a lot about how to study whales.

In studying animals that live in groups, scientists need to recognize individuals to see what each one does. Unique markings are used to identify individual whales. Scientists who study whales have learned to recognize specific humpbacks by the patterns of markings on their tails.

After coming to the surface for a breath of air, a humpback whale goes down by ducking its head deep into the

water and sticking its tail up into the air. Right then its tail fins, which are called *flukes*, are easy to see.

A good place to find lots of humpback whales is at their feeding grounds near Antarctica. In a study there, scientists made a catalog—like a class roll—from photographs of thirty-two whales' flukes.

Later in the year, the whales left Antarctica in their annual migration northward to breeding grounds in warmer waters. It is not easy to track a whale at sea. So the scientists didn't try. Instead, they went north to one of the breeding grounds and waited. The place they chose was in the Pacific Ocean near the coast of Colombia.

Late in August, the scientists found a big group of whales and began to make another catalog. They photographed one with fluke markings exactly like those of a whale in their catalog from Antarctica—it was the same whale. The first photo had been taken 131 days before the second one. That whale migrated 5,180 miles in less than five months. For mammals (if we don't count humans), that's a record.

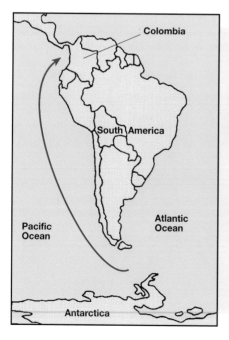

These are the tail fins of an amazing migrator. It was first spotted near Antarctica and was seen again near Colombia less than five months later.

How Birds Hatch Their Eggs

It's not easy.

I hope you have had the chance to see a pair of birds build a nest, hatch their eggs, and bring up their family. If you have, you know that they work pretty hard at it. A difficult part of that is just in hatching the eggs. In fact, that is so important that there have been studies to find out how it is done.

The first problem in hatching eggs is to hold them at just the right temperature. People who raise little chickens use heated incubators that keep the eggs at a steady temperature of 99 to 100 degrees Fahrenheit (F). That's close to your body temperature and just a little below a chicken's body temperature. At just a few degrees above or below this range, the eggs will not hatch.

Keeping their eggs at the right temperature is just as important for wild birds. Temperature measurements on incubating eggs for most kinds of birds fall in a range of 93 to 97 degrees F. That's a lot warmer than the usual outside temperature. You can see the problem: How do birds keep their eggs warm enough to hatch?

Most birds use body heat to keep their eggs warm. Just for the job of incubation they have spots of bare skin called *brood patches* on their undersides where they sit on the eggs. There are no feathers to slow down the flow of body heat to the eggs. Brood patches also allow birds to feel the eggs and check their temperatures. They can sit on the eggs "tightly" to make them warmer or more "loosely" if the eggs get too warm.

While the mother bird hunts for food, the temperature in her nest begins to drop . . .

The Problems of Hatching

Carefully sitting on a nest of eggs must get mighty tiresome during the two weeks or so needed to hatch them. How does a parent bird do that and still take time out to stretch a little and find enough food to make a living?

Different kinds of birds have different plans for doing this. In some plans both parents take turns sitting on the eggs. In some plans the female does it alone. In others the male does it alone. Still another plan is that one parent brings food to the other, which sits on the nest.

Female robins and house wrens do the hatching all by themselves and get their own food. That's also the plan used by a colony of weaverbirds living in an aviary in Los Angeles. Two scientists chose them for study because it was easy to get measuring equipment to their nests. They used

. . . so she returns to the nest again and again to warm up the eggs.

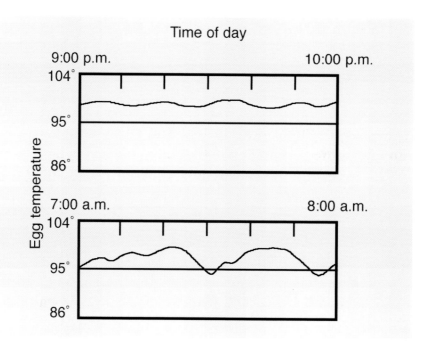

Time of day

9:00 p.m.

10:00 p.m.

104°

95°

86°

Egg temperature

7:00 a.m.

8:00 a.m.

104°

95°

86°

little electrical thermometers to get records of egg temperature during incubation. I have copied two of their records above.

The upper record was made between 9 and 10 o'clock at night, while a bird was continuously sitting on her nest. You can see that the eggs were held at an almost steady temperature partway between 95 and 104 degrees (actually 101 degrees F). All this time the parent bird was sitting on

the nest, keeping the temperature steady by adjusting the position of her brood patch.

The lower bumpy line is a part of the record made the following morning between 7 and 8 A.M. At first the scientists watched the bird as it made short trips away from the nest, mostly for food. It was easy to see that the temperature alone was all that was needed to tell when the bird left the nest and when she came back. We can tell that, too, just by looking at the record.

The temperature record reads from left to right. When the bird leaves her nest the line goes downward, telling that the eggs are beginning to cool toward the lower temperature outside. When the bird returns and begins sitting on her eggs again, the line goes upward as the eggs warm up toward her body temperature. You can count six places where the line slopes upward, showing that the bird came back to the nest.

Cold Days

The scientists continued recording the temperature day after day. When the outside temperature was colder, the record showed that the eggs cooled fast while the mama bird was away. The periods off the nest became shorter on colder days and the birds spent more time on the eggs to keep them warm. The bird must be able to feel the temperature of her eggs and manage her time on the nest to keep them warm enough.

Hatching eggs is a pretty big deal in the life of a pair of wild birds. They spend a lot of time and effort building a nest that is concealed or out of reach of predators and not far from a source of food. Then at least one of the birds must do the even harder job of paying attention to the eggs and keeping them warm until they hatch.

Why the Puffins Came Back to Egg Rock

After a hundred-year absence, they're back!

The people who brought them back were led by Dr. Stephen Kress. He is an *ornithologist*, a scientist who studies birds. In the early 1970s, he came to the Audubon camp on the Maine seacoast. In studying past records, he found that several kinds of seabirds had once nested on islands off the coast but were no longer there.

There had been a big colony of puffins nesting on a little island called Egg Rock. About a hundred years ago, people came to the island to take puffin eggs and trap the birds for their meat and feathers. Finally, the colony was destroyed, and the puffins never came back.

Steve studied up and learned a lot about puffins. They spend most of their lives at sea but do their nesting on islands scattered around the northern oceans. They need islands where they can find covered places for nests and where there are no rats or other predators. They are very social birds and like to live together in colonies. And they almost always return to nest on the same island on which they grew up.

Egg Rock looked like a great place for puffins. But how do you get a colony started if the birds always want to go back to the place where they grew up? Steve worked out a plan. It would take a lot of time and work.

First he got help from the Canadian Wildlife Service, which agreed to collect just-hatched puffin chicks from one of their big colonies. Six chicks were taken from a Canadian island to Egg Rock. Students served as assistants on the project and as parents for the chicks. They built nests out of blocks of sod, and they hand-fed small fish to the chicks three times a day.

Puffin Parents

After learning how to be puffin parents, the students began bringing up puffin chicks in greater numbers. Over the next seven years, a total of 774 chicks were brought to Egg Rock. The bringing-up part was successful. Most of the chicks grew up and were able to fly away when they were about seven weeks old. They had colored plastic leg bands to tell who they were.

Puffins spend their first two or three years at sea, often resting on the water like ducks. So the first of them were due back at Egg Rock in 1977. Would they come? And if they came, would they stay? Puffins have a strong need for togetherness. They don't like to be loners. Because only a small number of birds would return, there was a big worry that they might not stay. Steve and his helpers had decoys carved, hand painted, and set out on rock ledges. The decoys would make returning birds think they were joining a whole colony.

The first returning puffin was seen in June 1977 and was identified by its colored leg band. Others followed. But there was still one more worry. Even after returning, puffins cruise around and check out other islands for several summers. They do not mate and breed until they are about five years old. Would some of them nest on Egg Rock?

Success

The next big event came in 1981, when one of the assistants spotted a puffin with some fish in its beak flying to

Egg Rock. It scrambled across the rocks and delivered the fish to its nest.

That meant success. After almost a hundred years, puffins were breeding again at Egg Rock. Five pairs nested there in 1981. By 2000, thirty-five nesting pairs had made a stable, year-after-year colony.

Just to make sure it could be done again, Steve repeated the same process for a larger island, Seal Island. Over a six-year period, 950 puffin chicks were transplanted there. By 1994, 152 of them had lived through their time at sea and had been sighted in the neighborhood. By 2000, 126 breeding pairs were nesting on Seal Island.

Now that there are more colonies on different islands, it is less likely that puffins of the Maine seacoast could be wiped out by a disaster such as an oil spill. Stephen Kress and more than three hundred students who worked with him have made the Maine islands a safer place for puffins.

Tracking the Wandering Albatross

This bird spends most of its life on the wing.

The wandering albatross is a famous and mysterious bird that few of us ever see. Its fame began with sea stories in the days of sailing ships. Those few sailors who ventured into the stormy waters of the southern oceans had a story to tell. Their ship might be followed for days, even for weeks, by an albatross gliding close behind.

There have been scientific studies of the wandering albatross as an interesting bird with a special way of life. To start with, it's the largest sea bird, weighing about twenty pounds and with a wingspan often more than ten feet. Its long, narrow wings are better for gliding than for flapping.

The wandering albatross also has two tricks that allow it to spend most of its life on the wing. Gliding looks easier than flying. But just holding wings outstretched takes work by a bird's wing muscles. (Just try holding your arms outstretched for a few minutes. Even though you are not doing any useful work, your arm muscles will soon get tired.)

For the wandering albatross, gliding is easy because of a tricky wing design. A sheet of cartilage can lock and hold the wing in position so that gliding does not take much work.

Uplifting Air

The second trick has to do with ocean winds. Most gliding birds, like the hawks and buzzards, are high flyers. They glide on warm updrafts, or gusts of upward-blowing air.

The wandering albatross is a low flyer, usually skimming along a few feet above the waves. The waves are the key to the second trick. Ocean waves also make waves in the air above them. A wind blowing over the ocean surface has an upward swirl above every wave it passes.

You know about people who have fun using surfboards to ride the big ocean waves that come onto beaches. The wandering albatross is a wind surfer. It rides each little updraft that a wave gives to the wind blowing against it. Each updraft gives the bird enough lift to coast to the updraft of the next wave.

Once every two years, the wandering albatrosses return to the same lonely islands where they were born. Male and female of a pair have a big greeting ceremony and then get to the business of nest-building, mating, and egg-laying.

Then both parents take turns at the 40-day job of incubating the egg. After that comes a 280-day job of feeding the chick. Male and female go out on flights of several days looking for fish and squid to feed the chick. After the chick learns to fly, it goes off on its own lonely wander, and the parents go off on theirs.

The wandering albatross has never known predators. It has no fear of people and has been easy to study during its brief home life on land.

But how do you study an albatross when most of its life is spent wandering over the oceans? Two French scientists figured out how to track the birds for long flights during the nesting season.

They put little radio transmitters on several birds. Then they could locate the birds' positions every few hours by using radio receivers on two satellites. Observations from the satellites were sent to computers in France and used to draw a map of each bird's flight path.

On the map below, you can see the 33-day, 9,400-mile flight path of a male out searching for food while the female was home incubating an egg. Details of the map told a lot that had not been known.

By day, the albatross traveled distances up to 600 miles. At night, flights were much shorter, and the bird often stopped to rest on the surface. But it never rested for longer than a few hours at a time. It lived up to its reputation as a wanderer.

This map shows the flight path taken by a male wandering albatross during a 33-day period. It flew long distances each day and shorter ones at night, searching for food and sometimes swinging around the small islands of the southern Indian Ocean.

Africa

Area Shown

INDIAN OCEAN

Antarctica

When the Wind Dies

One kind of weather the albatross did not like was a dead calm with no wind at all. Then it would rest with only short flights, waiting for the wind to come. That need for wind explains why the wandering albatross lives where it does—only in the southern ocean around Antarctica, the windiest of all the seas.

Satellite tracking has taken away some, but not all, of the mystery from the wandering albatrosses. We can only wonder how these birds navigate and find their way where there are no signposts or landmarks. How do they travel thousands of miles on erratic or even zigzag courses, and how does each find its way home to a tiny speck of an island?

Living on the Edge of Danger

This ant loves heat.

Ants probably aren't your favorite insects. But you can't help being interested in the story of one spunky kind of ant. It has some special tricks for living in the hot, dry sands of the Sahara, in Africa. This desert is one of the most difficult places on earth for animals to make a living.

Most desert animals beat the heat by burrowing and living underground during the hottest part of the day. They come out to search for food at night and in the early morning. Of course, those animals include the predators, which come out at the same time to hunt. So ants and other small insects searching for their food are in danger of becoming food for larger animals, especially the desert lizards.

Head for Home

As the morning sun rises, the sands heat up rapidly and almost every creature scurries back to its burrow. Those that are still hungry and keep looking for food risk dying of heat shock before they get home.

Most desert ants and other insects head for home when the temperature gets up to about 95 degrees Fahrenheit. They must sneak past the ant lizards and win the race against rising temperature to get home safely. By the time the temperature gets to about 113 degrees, most ants are safe in their underground nests—except for one special kind, the Saharan silver ant.

The silver ant stays out in higher temperatures than any other desert ant does. In fact, it feeds on insects that died in the heat. What's its special strategy for survival?

Cool Tricks

One trick of the silver ant is that it can withstand higher temperatures—no one knows how—even up to 128 degrees.

And it knows how to find places where it can rest and cool off. Down on the surface of the sand, where the ant lives, is the hottest place around. Just a few inches up above the sand the air is a lot cooler. So the silver ant spends a part of its hunting time climbing up on plants, like the one in the picture on pages 42 and 43.

Silver ants have another trick that is even more surprising. Their whole colony stays in the nest until the sand temperature outside gets to about 116 degrees. Then a few scouts give a signal, and hundreds of ants come pouring out. This usually happens about noontime, when the temperature is rising rapidly.

Silver ants have a busy time of it, hunting and climbing up on grass stalks to cool off. Then they must hurry home again before the temperature gets to 128 degrees. That gives them just a short hunting time outside the nest, often only about ten minutes.

Naturally, you have to wonder why the silver ants don't come out of their nests until the temperature gets so high. Scientists who studied them wondered, too. They found an answer in the behavior of the ant lizard. It is especially fond of silver ants and often has its burrow close to one of their nests. But the ant lizard has to worry about getting overheated, too. By the time the temperature gets to 116 degrees, all the ant lizards are back in their burrows.

You can see why 116 degrees becomes a magic temperature for silver ants. When the desert sand gets that warm, one of their enemies, the ant lizard, is asleep in its burrow. Then the ants can safely go out hunting. Of course, their

safety doesn't last long. Their other enemy, the rising temperature, will tell them they must start for home before the sand gets to a killing temperature.

Lots of animals have special times of day or night when they do their hunting and searching for food. But there can't be very many that have as short a hunting time as the Saharan silver ant.

Many animals live very close to danger, especially those that live in the icy cold of the Arctic or in the hot, dry sands of the desert. Even so, the silver ant may hold some kind of record for living on the edge of danger. I think we should nominate it for an award.

When the desert heats up, silver ants often have only about ten minutes to hunt for food.

Second, the ant lizard stops hunting and goes into its burrow at about 116 degrees.

First, other ants head for home when the temperatures reach 95 to 113 degrees Fahrenheit.

Finally, the silver ant has a few minutes to come out and hunt— after the ant lizard goes home and before the temperature reaches 128 degrees.

The Seal Is a Sneaky Swimmer

A scientist caught it saving energy.

Terrie Williams was once a swimming instructor teaching people to swim. With practice, some people learn to be good swimmers, zipping through the water with ease.

But Terrie observed that, even with lots of practice, people must work hard and spend a great deal of energy in swimming. That observation led her to study other animal swimmers, from muskrats and otters to porpoises and seals. She has become an authority on marine mammals.

One of Terrie's favorite subjects is the common harbor seal, which is often seen as a trained performer at zoos and aquariums. Her seals were trained to swim against a current of water pumped through a water channel. For a swimmer, that activity is like walking or running on the moving belt of a treadmill. The swimmer stays in one place and can be connected up with wires and tubes to study his or her heart and breathing rates while swimming.

People swimming in the water channel behave just as they do during other forms of exercise. The heart beats faster to get more blood to working muscles. Both the breathing rate and the use of oxygen from the air increase with swimming speed to meet the muscles' increasing demand for oxygen.

Underwater Swimmers

Seals that swam in the water channel behaved very differently from people. At cruising speed, a seal spent only short spurts of three or four seconds swimming on the surface. While there, the seal would stick up its nose for a few quick breaths. In between breaths it spent much longer periods—about thirty seconds—submerged and swimming several feet below the surface.

This swimming pattern makes sense for the animal. A seal spends most of its life hunting for fish and squid far below the surface. Of course, it has a problem because it breathes air into lungs just as you do. So it must come to the surface to get air.

You may be wondering, just as I did, why a seal spends most of its time swimming below the surface, even when it is not hunting. The explanation lies in the behavior we see in any moving object. An object's motion is opposed by a force we call friction. For an object moving in water (or air) that frictional force is called *drag*. In swimming, that's the force that seems to be holding you back.

Now, it's a surprising fact that drag in water becomes greater if the object comes close to the surface. Anything moving on or close to the surface makes waves. And that takes extra energy.

Measuring Drag

Terrie and her team checked out this idea. They measured the drag that a seal must overcome in swimming. They did this by first training a group of seals to chomp down on a rubber mouthpiece that could be pulled by a rope. Then they measured the pounds of force on the rope when the seals were towed at different speeds both at the surface and submerged in a swimming pool.

As expected, the faster the seal was moving, the greater the drag force that worked against that movement. But even at the seal's low cruising speed of 3 miles per hour, drag at the surface was almost two times greater than the drag when submerged. At a higher speed of $4\frac{1}{2}$ miles an hour the surface drag was almost three times greater than the submerged drag. Terrie concluded that swimming below the surface must be a lot easier. Seals are no dummies. They probably discovered this early in their lives.

The Seal's Routine

So the seal has a special swimming routine: quick breaths at the surface, then a longer swim underneath. That is possible because of some features of its body machinery. At the surface, the seal's heart revs up extra fast, to as many as 140 beats a minute. It is pumping blood past the fresh air in its lungs.

The seal can hold a big supply of oxygen. Its body has a lot more blood than yours does. And the blood has more red hemoglobin, which carries oxygen. Even the seal's muscles are extra red with a special hemoglobin that gives them an extra oxygen storehouse. Just a few seconds of swimming at the surface loads up the seal's body with enough oxygen for a long underwater swim.

Terrie Williams has discovered how seals can be sneaky swimmers.

Why You Can't Beat a Seal

• Your body can't store as much oxygen for swimming underwater.
• With your knees and elbows sticking out, you have lots more drag than a seal, which is streamlined. So even for slow swimming you have to spend energy three times as fast as a seal does.

A Cool Story About an Antarctic Fish

Why doesn't it freeze?

The key word is *ice*.

That describes the ocean around the edges of Antarctica. Far from land, a giant shelf of ice meets the ocean. At the underside of the shelf, a jumble of crushed ice and slush provides a home to a world of algae and tiny animals. In that icy soup there also lives a small fish, the Antarctic cod.

For forty years scientists have been curious about that fish. How does it live where most fish would freeze to death? It must have some secret. The Antarctic is not a comfortable place to work, so research has been slow in solving the problem. Now it seems we finally have an answer.

Research was begun by cutting holes in the ice and catching the fish with hook and line. Scientists studied the fish's blood and measured its freezing point, the temperature at which ice crystals just begin to form.

The fish were taken from seawater that had a temperature of 28.6 degrees Fahrenheit (F) and many ice crystals floating in it. The blood did not begin to freeze until its temperature was lowered to 28.3 degrees F. That small difference is enough that the fish can live at the freezing temperature of the ice-salt mixture.

The scientists' next research job was clear: Find out what kind of stuff in the fish's blood kept it from freezing. Their search led to some really weird stuff made up of a protein never before seen in the blood of a fish. When this stuff was removed, the blood froze at the same temperature as seawater. When it was put back, the blood again had its antifreeze character and a lowered freezing point.

Making Ice

Before deciding what to do next, the scientists thought about what happens to water when it freezes. That process takes place molecule by molecule. Water molecules easily moving around as a liquid suddenly become locked into position in an ice crystal.

In pure water, freezing begins to happen when the water is cooled to 32.0 degrees F, which is its freezing point. Anything dissolved in the water is made up of atoms or molecules, which get in the way of water molecules. By crowding in, they make it harder for water molecules to lock together into an ice crystal. That lowers the freezing point.

Lots of substances can be used as antifreezes. *Ethylene glycol* works well in the radiators of automobile engines. Another antifreeze, so cheap that we use it in winter on roads and sidewalks, is plain old table salt. Seawater has enough salt to lower its freezing point to 28.6 degrees F.

Melting is just the opposite of freezing. It happens when water molecules get warm enough and zippy enough to bounce out of ice crystals and move around as liquid water. The lowest temperature at which that begins to happen is the melting point.

For water and for solutions of most substances, scientists take the melting point and freezing point to be the same temperature. Only a tiny temperature change determines whether ice crystals are forming or melting.

Super Antifreeze

It was easy to find out that the new fish protein must be very different from any known antifreeze. Its molecules are about a hundred times more effective than salt molecules in lowering the temperature needed to form ice crystals. And the crystals that do form take on oddball shapes.

The strangest thing about this new protein antifreeze is that it lowers the freezing point but not the melting point. Blood that has the antifreeze in it will not freeze above 28.3 degrees. Once that same blood is frozen, it will not begin to melt at 28.3 degrees. The blood will not melt until it goes all the way up to 32 degrees again. This is a big surprise, and means the stuff works in some way that scientists don't yet understand.

Study of the molecular structure of the fish antifreeze shows that it is an unusual kind of protein. It has many

Antarctic cod

small sugar molecules held in special positions within each big protein molecule. Because of its sugar content, it is called a *glycoprotein*. So it has come to be called the antifreeze fish glycoprotein, or *AFGP*.

There is one more part to the story of AFGP: How does it work to be such a powerful antifreeze?

We don't yet have a complete explanation, but we do have a pretty good idea. Chemists have learned to tell a lot about the behavior of a molecule just from its structure. Their idea is that the sugar groups are all on one side of the molecule.

Sugars are so sticky to water molecules that they are called "water-loving" groups. They stick to the water molecules at the surface of an ice crystal.

The other side of the AFGP molecule has only "water-hating" groups. They tend to stay away from water, to stay dry. That gives the ice crystal a dry surface and makes it hard for water molecules to attach to an ice crystal.

You can see that it's easy to think of AFGP preventing

the growth of ice crystals and the freezing of water. Of course, this is just an idea yet to be proven. So there is still something more to be learned from fish that swim among ice crystals.

Other Fish Antifreezes

There is another question you might ask about ice-cold fish: How about fish in the waters near the North Pole? Fish of the Arctic Ocean also have antifreeze proteins. There are at least three different kinds. They do not contain sugars, but they all have the same kind of antifreeze effects. It seems that the invention of antifreeze in fish happened more than once.

Warm-Blooded Fish?

Some fish can keep parts of their bodies warm.

If you've ever jumped into a cold lake for a swim, you know how rapidly your body can lose heat to the cold water, even when you're trying to stay warm.

Most fish don't even try to stay warm. Their bodies are only slightly warmer than the water they swim in. Since they breathe water, they would have a big problem trying to warm up. Fish get their oxygen from the water around them by pumping blood through tiny vessels in their gills. As the blood goes through the gills, it picks up a full load of oxygen. The blood also comes to the same temperature as the water. You can see why a fish living in cold water is about as cold-blooded as an animal can get.

Cold-blooded animals have an advantage in that they don't have to use energy to keep warm. So they don't need much food. But when they do get cold, they are likely to be sluggish. Their body machinery slows down, and they can't swim or think as fast.

A few fish have ways to get around the temperature problem. The swordfish, for example, has a special built-in heater that warms the blood going to its eyes and brain. The heater is made of tissue that looks like muscle but can't contract. The tissue spends all of its energy just to make heat. The heater allows the swordfish to go down into deep, cold water in search of prey.

Bluefin Tuna

The Tuna's Tricks

Tuna have a more complicated series of inventions. A large tuna is a marathon swimmer and can keep going at speeds of almost 9 miles an hour for long periods. It swims with a tail motion that is worked by a big slab of muscle. That hard-working muscle generates a lot of heat. In most other kinds of fish, this heat is lost when blood from the muscle goes back to the gills for another load of oxygen. But the tuna has a special trick that saves some heat.

Close to the muscle is a place where warm blood from the muscle goes past cold blood coming in from the gills. The two bloodstreams race past each other in tiny thin-walled tubes. An engineer would call that a *countercurrent heat exchanger*.

Swordfish

The heat exchanger uses blood that is leaving the muscle to warm the incoming blood. In bluefin tuna, muscle temperatures may be more than 25 degrees Fahrenheit above the outside water temperature.

The bluefin's brain is kept warm by a similar small heat exchanger. Because it has these two systems, one scientist has called the bluefin tuna an *endotherm*: a warm-blooded animal.

In-Between Cases

No fish can keep its body warm the way you do. But that may be the most interesting part of all. We have been used to thinking that all animals had to be either warm-blooded endotherms or cold-blooded *ectotherms*. But some fish are in-between cases—just a part of the body is kept warm. So it seems that the inventions for keeping warm can occur in stages.

If you are a dinosaur fan, then you might know of the arguments about whether the dinosaurs were warm-blooded or cold-blooded. Now you can see that there are in-between possibilities. Maybe some dinosaurs, like some fish, kept only parts of their bodies warm.

High-Tech Fish

They have their own electric fields.

Of the world's thousands of kinds of fish, a few hundred are electric fish. I call them high-tech because just studying them requires some of our most advanced technology. These fish are found in the river systems of Africa and South America.

Electric fish have a wide range of electrical abilities. There is an electric eel that can stun its prey with a shock of five hundred volts. It is called a *strongly electric* fish. The many kinds of *weakly electric* fish are more common. They produce low voltages to sense their surroundings.

I got into electric fish by a happy accident. In a laboratory next to mine at the University of Texas in Austin, I saw a man counting out earthworms. I asked if he was going fishing. "No," he said, "I'm getting ready to feed my fish." His name was Troy Smith. He had come for advanced studies with my friend Harold Zakon, who is an old hand with electric fish. They were studying *neurobiology*—how nerves work—and are using electric fish in their experiments.

Troy's aquarium holds about a dozen of his pets—long, skinny knife-shaped fish of various sizes up to a foot long. Their official name is *Sternopygus* (ster-NOP-ih-gus). They swim slowly—sometimes forward, sometimes backward—by the rippling motion of feathery fins on their undersides.

Troy had a little gadget on a long plastic rod. It was connected to an amplifier and loudspeaker. When it was held in the water near a fish, we could hear an electrical signal as a steady hum at 73 beats per second.

"That's a male," Troy told me. "The females have a hum with higher frequency, usually over 100."

With that introduction, I began studying up on electric fish, first by reading so I could talk to Troy and Harold about them. Here's the story: first the big idea and then how the electric sense really works.

A Cloud of Charges

The idea is that a fish creates an electric field around itself consisting of two clouds of electric charges. Then by sensing the density of the cloud, the fish can tell about anything in the way. How a fish can do all that takes us into many different parts of science.

Sternopygus has an electric organ at the base of its tail. The organ is made of neat and regular stacks of cells that look like muscle cells when seen under a microscope. Instead of doing mechanical work as cells in muscle do, all their energy goes into making electricity.

Each cell in the electric organ makes only a tiny voltage, but when they are stacked together they give voltages high enough to be useful. The electricity does not come out into the water as a steady current. Instead, it has a very regular on-off pattern. When recorded, as you can see in the graph on page 60, each fish has its own different pattern or "signature."

The water around a fish can carry electricity only because the water contains some salts dissolved from rocks and soil. And in water, salts always split apart to form oppositely charged particles, or *ions*.

In chemical language, ordinary table salt is sodium chloride. It's written in shorthand as *NaCl*. But in water, salt occurs only as positive sodium ions ($Na+$) and negative chloride ions ($Cl-$).

The fish's electric organ works just like an electric battery.

The fish's electric field is in the form of two clouds of electric charges around it. The fish can feel anything that gets in the way or changes the clouds of electric charges.

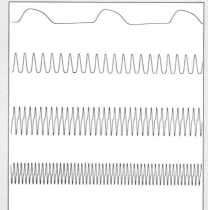

The regular on-off patterns recorded for four different kinds of weakly electric fish show great variety. By recognizing distinctive patterns, electric fish can tell whether another fish is a friend or enemy.

It pulls positive ions toward one end and negative ions toward the other. This action creates two clouds of electric charges around the fish.

An Electric Sense

To sense those electric clouds around it, the fish has a regular pattern of special nerve endings called *electro-receptors* in its skin. Each one works as a tiny voltmeter to tell about the density of the electric cloud right outside.

All together, the nerve messages tell the brain about the shape of the electric cloud and about anything—like a rock or a plant or another fish—that changes the cloud's shape. Its electric sense gives *Sternopygus* a way to "feel" things nearby even without touching them.

Electric Language

Some interesting things happen when a number of electric fish get together. When two fish are making electric patterns that are almost the same, one fish will change its timing so that the two patterns do not interfere with each other.

Since the fish can sense one another's electrical patterns, they also have a special way to communicate. Scientists have "listened in" and recorded the electrical signatures, then played them back to other fish. Two kinds of messages were easy for the scientists to read. Even at a distance and in the dark, an electric fish can tell the difference between a friendly neighbor and a threatening stranger.

Electric fish are studied partly out of curiosity to understand their special sense and how it works. A more practical reason is that their electrical signature is very closely tied to the nervous system that controls it. Usually nerves and the muscles they control are buried deep down inside skin, muscles, or other tissues. But nerve control of the electric organ is easy to study because the nerve endings are right at the surface. So *Sternopygus* provides a good place to study how nerves work.

I think it's a cool part of science that fish from a muddy tropical river should help us learn about how nerves work.

BIBLIOGRAPHY

Elephant Talk
Payne, K.B., W.R. Langbauer Jr., and E.M. Thomas. 1986. Infrasonic calls of the Asian elephant. *Behavioral Ecology and Sociobiology* 18:297–301.

Poole, J.H., K. Payne, W.R. Langbauer Jr., and C.J. Moss. 1988. The social contexts of some very low frequency calls of African elephants. *Behavioral Ecology and Sociobiology* 22:385–392.

Do Dogs See in Color?
Neitz, J., T. Geist, and G.H. Jacobs. 1989. Color vision in the dog. *Visual Neuroscience* 3:119–125.

How Dogs Came from Wolves
Morey, D.F. 1994. Early evolution of the domestic dog. *American Scientist* 82:336–347.

Trut, L.N. 1999. Early canid domestication: the farm-fox experiment. *American Scientist* 87:160–169.

The Long-Distance Whale
Stone, G.S., L. Florez-Gonzalez, and S. Katona. 1990. Whale migration record. *Nature* 346:705.

How Birds Hatch Their Eggs
Dent, R. Incubation. In: *Avian Biology*, D.S. Farmer, J.R. King, and K.C. Parker, eds. New York: Academic Press, 1975.

White, F.N., and J.L. Kinney. 1974. Avian incubation. *Science* 186:107–114.

Why the Puffins Came Back to Egg Rock
Kress, S.W. 1992. From Puffins to Petrels. *Living Bird* 11:14–19.

Tracking the Wandering Albatross
Jouventin, P., and H. Weimerskirch. 1990. Satellite tracking of the wandering albatross. *Nature* 343:746–748.

Living on the Edge of Danger
Wehner, R., A.C. Marsh, and S. Wehner. 1992. Desert ants on a thermal tightrope. *Nature* 357:596–597.

The Seal Is a Sneaky Swimmer
Williams, T.M., G.L. Kooyman, and D.H. Kroll. 1991. Effect of submergence on heart rate and oxygen consumption of swimming seals and sea lions. *Journal of Comparative Physiology* B 160:637–644.

Williams, T.M., and G.L. Kooyman. 1985. Swimming performance and hydrodynamic characteristics of harbor seals. *Physiological Zoology* 58:576–589.

A Cool Story About an Antarctic Fish
DeVries, A.L. Freezing resistance in fishes. In: *Fish Physiology*, W.S. Hoar and D.J. Randall, eds. New York: Academic Press, 1971.

Raymond, J.A., and A.L. DeVries. 1977. Adsorption inhibition as a mechanism of freezing resistance in polar fishes. *Proceedings of the National Academy of Sciences USA* 74:2589–2593.

Warm-Blooded Fish?
Holland, K.M., R.W. Brill, R.K.C. Chang, J.R. Sibert, and D.A. Fournier. 1992. Physiological and behavioral thermoregulation in bigeye tuna. *Nature* 358:410–412.

High-Tech Fish
Moller, P. *Electric Fishes*. London: Chapman and Hall, 1995.

INDEX